Super Cat

Super Cat

Super Cat Saves the Day

EMMA OLIVER

Super Cat sped through the air, his cape flowing out behind him.

He was hurrying to get to the park to find out which Dog was causing chaos.

A worried mummy bunny had alerted Super Cat, saying that a naughty Dog was terrifying the little bunnies that were having fun in the park.

When he landed at the gate of the park, he saw who he was going to have to do battle with.

It was Dog Danger, a mean baddie who was always frightening the baby rabbits.

"Dog Danger, I have come to ask you nicely to leave the bunnies alone! They were playing nicely until you arrived."

"Ha ha ha ha, Super Cat. I just love terrifying these bunnies. It's so much fun!" Dog Danger said. He turned to the bunnies and growled at them.

Super Cat looked over towards the bunnies and saw that they had all gone back to their mummies to hide behind them for safety.

"Leave now, Dog Danger, or I will zap you with my powers," said Super Cat, getting ready to zap Dog Danger with his laser eyes.

"You don't scare me, kitty cat," scorned Dog Danger. His laughter boomed across the park, scaring away any other animal who was watching.

"I'll give you one last chance..."

"Or what?" growled Dog Danger.

"Or I will zap you."

"Ha ha ha ha!" Dog Danger laughed then gave a massive snarl and charged towards Super Cat.

Luckily, Super Cat was prepared and was able to zap Dog Danger before he got too close.

The zap from Super Cat knocked Dog Danger over and made him whimper.
He scowled at Super Cat before running off out of the park.

The mummy rabbits and the little bunnies were so happy now that Dog Danger was gone.
"Hooray for Super Cat!" they all chanted.

A little bunny came up to Super Cat and said,
"Thank you, Mr Super Cat, for protecting us."

Super Cat smiled down at the bunny and patted its head.
"I will always protect my town, no matter what," replied Super Cat.

The bunny smiled and hopped back to his mummy. The bunnies started playing in the park again and the mummy rabbits were happy again.

Super Cat smiled to himself, knowing he had done a good job.

"Well, everyone, my work here is done. Goodbye for now, and stay safe."

"Goodbye, Super Cat," everyone replied.

Super Cat waved and took off into the air. He flew back to his base to await his next mission to sort out those naughty Dogs.